All Sorts
to Make a World

All Sorts
to Make a World

John Agard

With illustrations by
Michael Broad

Barrington Stoke

For Marcus, Kalera, Lesley and Yansan –
grandson and daughters posse

First published in 2014 in Great Britain by
Barrington Stoke Ltd
18 Walker Street, Edinburgh, EH3 7LP

www.barringtonstoke.co.uk

Text © 2014 John Agard
Illustrations © 2014 Michael Broad

This story was first published in a different form in
Ip Dip Sky Blue (Collins, 1990)

The moral right of John Agard and Michael Broad to be
identified as the author and illustrator of this work has
been asserted in accordance with the Copyright, Designs
and Patents Act, 1988

A CIP catalogue record for this book is available
from the British Library upon request

ISBN: 978-1-78112-370-6

Printed in China by Leo

Contents

Chapter 1
Inner City Stress

It was one of those grey, wet London days, when you feel you could disappear into your coat or anorak, and a girl named Shona was travelling with her dad on the Underground.

Shona and her dad were on their way home from the Natural History Museum where they had been to see the displays on evolution.

It was Shona's half-term holiday, but her dad called their day out "an educational outing". It would help Shona with her school project on how the human race evolved.

Shona had had more fun with the flying dinosaurs than the ancestors of humankind, but she'd written down words like "Hominids" and "Neanderthals" and "Homo Sapiens" in her new little notebook.

Shona felt the Neanderthals looked too serious for her liking. But perhaps it was a serious business to be a hunter-gatherer. The face of one of the Neanderthals reminded Shona of her headmaster, but she wouldn't write that in her project.

Shona loved the 3D animated image of Lucy, a female fossil-skeleton who had been discovered in Ethiopia. As they stood before her, Shona's dad smiled. "Lucy is one of us," he said. "The human race is her extended family. Come to think of it, she reminds me of someone we both know. Your granny."

Shona wasn't sure how her granny would take that, but she loved Lucy's wise, dreamy face that seemed to contain all the human story. Shona felt as if Lucy's skeleton was peering into the heart of modern folks from across a distance of more than three million years.

"But," Shona asked her dad, "why was she called Lucy? Like my best friend at school," she added. "If Lucy was discovered in Africa, then how come she doesn't have an African name?"

Shona's dad said that the team who found Lucy were celebrating back in their camp, and it just so happened that the Beatles song "Lucy in the Sky with Diamonds" was playing on the radio at that very moment.

So, in her notebook, Shona wrote that Lucy in the earth was named after Lucy in the sky. And next to the word "Beatles", she wrote the word "bi-pedal" to remind her that Lucy walked on two legs.

Shona's dad was impressed and told her some more facts for her notebook. "The Beatles didn't have the last word when it came to Lucy's name," he said. "In her homeland of

Ethiopia, where her skeleton rests now, she is called Dinknesh."

"Dinknesh," said Shona. "That's beautiful."

"Yes," said her dad, "and its meaning is beautiful too – it means Amazing One."

Shona and her dad were so busy chatting that, when they reached the Underground station, they went to the wrong platform and found themselves on the Victoria line.

"Never mind, we can change at Green Park for the Piccadilly line," her dad said.

On the Underground, nobody else seemed to be in a talking or smiling mood, so Shona whispered to her dad, "Why is everybody so serious?"

Shona didn't know how to whisper easy. She whispered so loud that a man in a grey pinstripe suit and red braces looked up from his pink newspaper.

"Must be all the stress and the cold," her dad said.

"What stress?" Shona asked.

"Stress," her dad said. "Inner city stress."

Shona saw her dad smile as he said "inner city stress", and she could tell from the look behind the silver frames of his specs that he must be making up some story in his head.

Shona's dad was always telling her stories. Whenever Shona had trouble falling asleep, he'd get her to count the beads in her hair. Beads like smiling seeds all over her plaited hair. "Better than counting sheep," he told her.

Then he'd say, "Sleep tight, Shining Beads Girl."

Shona liked to think of Shining Beads Girl as her secret name. Wouldn't it be great if everybody in the world had a secret name?

Like a password nobody could guess.

'Even our ancestors,' Shona thought, 'have their secret names.' She thought of how her granny shared a wise, dreamy face with Dinknesh-Lucy. Perhaps her granny's secret name might be something like Dreamy Wise Eye.

But right now, Shining Beads Girl was counting how many more stops they had left to get to Wood Green, which was a long way along the Piccadilly line. They had just passed Green Park, so there were at least another nine stops to go, and Shona wished something interesting would happen to brighten up the journey.

Chapter 2
The Tube

Darkness rattled past the train windows and then a fellow with pierced lips and loads of tattoos got on. Dragons danced on his upper arms and thick black patterns swirled along down his forearms. They made his skin look like the long sleeves of his T-shirt.

Tattoo Fellow plonked himself beside Pinstripe Man and started to roll up a ciggy. He took his time licking the roll-up paper and for a moment he pretended he was about to light up.

"Just you dare, just you dare!" was all Pinstripe Man said from behind his newspaper.

Tattoo Fellow shrugged him off. "Only winding you up, mate," he said. "Don't get your braces in a twist."

Just then the train came to a stop. Doors slid open, as usual. Doors slid shut, as usual. People got on and off, as usual.

It wasn't busy like the rush hour, so at least the train wasn't packed. Shona hated it when everybody was squashed together. 'Maybe that's why they call it the Tube,' she thought. Like a squashy tube of toothpaste. But not so nice-smelling. Not like mint. More like sweat.

Somehow two teenage boys managed to wriggle their way between the doors as they closed. They were both holding a skateboard under one arm and playing loud music on their mobiles.

"The iPod Twins have just landed on planet earth!" Shona's dad whispered. Trust Dad to say something like that. But in a funny sort of way he was right. One boy was white and the other black, but they were both wearing identical green caps turned backwards and baggy trousers. They even had the same colour trainers.

And, from the sound of it, they were listening to identical music – music that filled the train with a wild buzz.

The iPod Twins had indeed landed and were about to prove that they could balance on a skateboard on a moving train and at the same time shake their heads to a buzzing beat.

A woman in a dark blue skirt and white blouse looked up from her Kindle, as if she was about to say something. Shona wondered how it felt to read a book with pages you couldn't turn or smell, but Kindle Woman seemed lost in her screen-book, at least until the iPod Twins landed in her private space, not with a crash, but with an almighty buzz.

So Kindle Woman rolled her eyes at Pinstripe Man, who gave a little cough, or perhaps a little grunt.

'Maybe that's what music does to grown-ups,' Shona thought. 'Some cough or grunt. Some roll their eyes. Some nod their chins.'

Shona would rather tap her feet. The way her dad was tapping his at that very moment.

Across from Dad, an old lady in a purple shawl kept stroking the ear of a small, mousey-faced dog that was whimpering in her lap. "Never mind, Bessie," the old lady said to comfort the dog. "Never mind, it's only music coming out of that mobile thingy. It won't hurt yah."

"Call that music?" Pinstripe Man chimed in. "Sounds more like a swarm of ballistic bees!"

"In my teen days, it was the ghetto blaster," Shona's dad said. "We used to pump up the volume. The old ghetto blaster would have had this train sounding like a dance hall."

Shona groaned. Any chance he got, her dad would chat on about his raving teen days.

"I seem to remember it was called a Brixton Briefcase," Kindle Woman said, speaking out of the blue to Shona's dad.

Shona saw a shadow of a smile on Kindle Woman's lips. She wondered whether Kindle Woman was flirting with her dad. He was smiling back. "These days you got to be careful how you say things like Brixton Briefcase," he said. "Don't broadcast this, but I still have a ghetto blaster in the attic."

The iPod Twins rolled their eyes and whispered "Dinosaur" loud enough for everyone to hear. Then they turned up their music.

"Not so loud, dearies," the old lady said, with a thin-lip smile. "My doggie, Bessie, likes her music soft, and the sound of bees scares the life out of her. Isn't that true, Bessie?"

But the iPod Twins blanked the old lady and carried on as if they were the only people in the universe that mattered.

Chapter 3
Stuck

"Flip me, we're stuck!" Tattoo Fellow said all of a sudden.

"Good lord, you're right," Pinstripe Man replied. "I do believe we are stuck."

It seemed that for once Pinstripe Man agreed with Tattoo Fellow. Yes, the train was not going forward and it was not going backward.

They were stuck in an Underground tunnel, that was for sure. Stuck with each other.

Silence.

Pinstripe Man looked at his watch.

Kindle Woman texted someone on her mobile.

Shona took out a packet of bubble gum from her anorak pocket.

Tattoo Fellow did a funny impression of Pinstripe Man's posh voice, as if he was telling Shona off.

"Just you dare, just you dare, young lady. This is a no-bubble-gum-chewing zone. I'm

afraid it's illegal to pollute the air with your bubbles."

Pinstripe Man shifted in his seat, but Shona could tell Tattoo Fellow was only joking.

"Won't be long, Bessie, won't be long," the old lady kept saying to her dog, stroking its ear all the while.

Chapter 4
Say Something in Yellow

As they all sat there and wondered in silence, the door between their carriage and the next one opened.

In walked a very short old man dressed all in yellow and holding a yellow umbrella.

A yellow hankie was tucked into his yellow coat pocket and you could see yellow socks peeping out from under yellow trousers.

The old man sat down without a word. He propped his hands on the handle of his yellow umbrella and began to whistle to himself.

Shona thought he looked a bit spooky, in a friendly sort of way.

But maybe he was just a lonely old man who'd seen so much grey around him – grey clouds, grey buildings, grey coats – that he decided to say something to the world in yellow.

Shona thought about how much he must like yellow. She imagined that his favourite flower was bound to be daffodil. And she wouldn't be at all surprised if he also dreamed in yellow.

"Bet he lives in a yellow submarine," Shona's dad whispered.

Shona remembered her dad belting out that song about a yellow submarine on his ghetto blaster. It was one of those songs that he liked to call "an oldie".

And his whisper wasn't as soft as he thought, for Kindle Woman smiled across at him again. "I see you know the Beatles," she said. "And it's clear you're not shy about your age."

"I'm shy about many things," Dad replied. "But I'm not shy about showing my age."

Shona decided that Kindle Woman did fancy her dad.

And all the while they were chatting, the old man kept up his soft whistling.

And all the while, the train still wasn't going anywhere.

Then Tattoo Fellow pointed to the bright yellow scarf. With a smile on his face, he asked the old man which football team he supported.

The old man replied in a high, sing-song sort of voice.

"I support the joy of life, my friend, but I don't suppose you've heard of that team. By the way, my name is Doctor Bananas and I never travel in a no-laughing carriage. I whistle to meself. Don't need a ticket to whistle to yourself, do you?"

Nobody said anything. Not even Tattoo Fellow.

Chapter 5
Bananas in Space

Everyone sat, saying nothing, and pretended not to listen to Doctor Bananas as he whistled his old-fashioned songs.

All of a sudden, Doctor Bananas stopped whistling and looked round at them.

"Have any of you good people heard of the monkey who went bananas in space?" he asked. "Serves them right for putting a monkey on a spaceship. Never consulted the poor monkey, did they? Are there any bananas on Mars, I ask you. Haven't they poisoned the fish and the seals enough? Now they're after the bananas in space. Like I always say, a banana a day keeps the doctor away. But the truth is that no one has the right to plunder the bananas that grow in space."

The old man spoke very fast, as if he didn't need to pause for breath.

Then he pulled out his hankie and shook it in the air.

From out of nowhere, a banana appeared in his hand.

'It's like a magic show,' Shona thought.

Shona had seen magicians pull a rabbit out of a hat. But she'd never seen a banana appear out of a hankie. Shona felt certain that this Doctor Bananas must be some kind of magician. Even if she had heard the iPod Twins whisper "Weirdo!" to each other when he did the banana trick.

Doctor Bananas peeled the banana with care, ate it, and put the skin into his coat pocket.

"I always take my litter home with me. Do you?" he asked Pinstripe Man, who looked completely taken by surprise.

"I should jolly well say I do," was all Pinstripe Man said.

"And I should jolly well hope so too," Doctor Bananas said, and he pointed his umbrella at Pinstripe Man. The way he was pointing that yellow umbrella made Shona think it was some kind of magic wand or a baton to conduct an invisible orchestra.

"Well, I must love you and leave you," Doctor Bananas said. "I'm off to visit some other folks stuck in the middle of a tunnel. No

forward, no backward. Stuck in the same boat.
Stuck in the same tunnel. That's life. Nothing
to do but face each other. Good bananas to you,
my friends. Good bananas till we meet again."

And just so, Doctor Bananas disappeared into the next carriage.

Chapter 6
A Jumbie Story

When Doctor Bananas had gone, everyone looked around at one another, as if they weren't sure what had just happened.

The hum of the not-moving train reminded Shona that they were not dreaming.

Then they all spoke at once.

"Funny geezer," Tattoo Fellow said.

"Nutter," the iPod Twins said.

"Like a character out of a mind-mangling novel," Kindle Woman said.

"Well, it takes all sorts to make a world," the old lady with the dog said.

But Shona had her eyes on Pinstripe Man, for all of a sudden he wasn't looking very well.

He put one hand to his head as if he had a headache coming on.

"I'm beginning to feel a bit short of breath," Pinstripe Man said. He took out a yellow hankie from his coat pocket and fanned away at himself. "I must say, the lack of air is driving me bananas."

Shona offered him some bubble gum, but Pinstripe Man said a polite, "No thank you."

36

"Then would you like my dad to tell you a ghost story?" Shona asked, being very polite too.

"No thank you," Pinstripe Man said again, this time with the hint of a smile.

But before you could say "crick-crack", Shona's dad had begun a West Indian jumbie story about a Jack-o-Lantern and his flickering yellow lights.

"That's awfully nice of you to tell me a story," Pinstripe Man said. "But a ghost story isn't quite what I need just now, thank you."

But Shona's dad was well into his storytelling element and Shona knew nothing could stop him now, not even the worried looks from Pinstripe Man.

As he spoke, Shona's dad pulled his specs down to the tip of his nose, to make sure everyone could see those sparkling, greenish cat-eyes.

He liked to tell Shona those eyes were thanks to the Irish somewhere in his African blood. Shona's dad's born-island was Montserrat. He'd told Shona all about how Montserrat was the only island in the Caribbean with a golden Irish harp on its flag. And about how it was the only place in the world outside of Ireland that had St Patrick's Day as a national holiday.

"Slavery and exile threw African and Irish into the same boat," Shona's dad had told her many a time. "But that's not a history anyone would want to repeat."

He'd often tell Shona scary jumbie stories, too. He'd turn himself into characters like Jack-o-Lantern, who he also called Spooky Lights. In his stories, Spooky Lights liked nothing better than to lead travellers astray over bushes and bogs with his devilish flickering lanterns.

Now you see him, now you don't. That was Spooky Lights all right.

And right now, on a going-nowhere train, stuck with strangers in silence, Shona's dad was doing his best Spooky Lights voice.

Pinstripe Man hid behind his newspaper.

Kindle Woman seemed transfixed by Shona's dad's antics.

"How about a little music?" the iPod Twins asked, and they grabbed the moment to blast out their sounds.

This time Pinstripe Man didn't object to the buzzing. In fact, he turned to the old lady with the dog and said, "I see your Bessie isn't too bothered by the music now. She's even wagging her tail."

"I always knew my Bessie had an ear for music," the old lady replied. "You do, don't you, Bessie?"

Then Pinstripe Man reached across and tickled Bessie behind the ears.

"Good lord, don't know what's come over me, but I'm peckish all of a sudden, and I do believe a banana a day keeps the doctor away."

With that, Pinstripe Man opened his briefcase on his knees. The last thing anybody expected him to bring out was a big yellow banana, but that's exactly what he did.

He started to eat the banana with as much care as he'd folded his newspaper.

"I always take my litter home with me," he said, and he put the skin into his briefcase. "Anyone for a banana?" he asked. He looked round the carriage and took yet another banana from his briefcase.

Tattoo Fellow looked on in amazement. "How many bananas you got in there, mate?" he couldn't help asking.

"You never know, my young friend, you never know," Pinstripe Man said. "Life is full of surprises. There may even be bananas on Mars, for all we know."

At that moment, Shona felt a strange lightness creep over their carriage. Even the dragons on Tattoo Fellow's arms seemed to be smiling.

Chapter 7
Sharing Secrets

Nobody moaned or seemed to mind any more that the train had been stood still for 15 minutes. They were all stuck in the same pickle together. The sound of laughter was soon echoing down the tunnel.

When at last the train was on the move again, Pinstripe Man stood up to get off at the next stop, King's Cross.

"Good lord," he said. "Looks like the old fellow has forgotten his umbrella. I guess I'm by duty bound to take it to the Lost and Found."

And he gave Shona a funny look, as if they were sharing a secret.

Then, with a very dignified, "Good bananas, folks, till we meet again," Pinstripe Man vanished into the crowd on the station platform.

Shona watched him go.

She had to admit that Pinstripe Man looked an odd sight, with a leather briefcase in one hand and a bright yellow umbrella in the other.

When at long last Shona and her dad arrived at Wood Green, Shona noticed that Kindle Woman got off at the same stop as them.

But first she smiled at Shona's dad. "Our paths may yet cross again," she said. "So here's to Spooky Lights."

Shona's dad smiled back. "You can always look me up in the Yellow Pages under Jack-o-Lantern!"

Then, with a few brisk steps, Kindle Woman had vanished.

Shona thought what a day it had turned out to be. "An educational outing," as her dad had said.

Shona had walked among Neanderthals and she'd jumped across millions of years to meet with the iPod Twins, Kindle Woman, Tattoo Fellow and of course Pinstripe Man, not to mention Doctor Bananas.

All sorts of people. What would Dinknesh-Lucy, the wonderful fossil skeleton, make of a day like this?

More *4u2read* titles ...

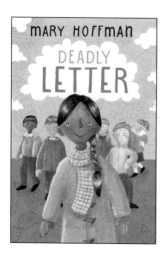

Deadly Letter
MARY HOFFMAN

"Ip dip sky blue.
Who's it? Not you."

Prity wants to play with the other children at school, but it's hard when you're the new girl and you don't know the rules. And it doesn't help when you're saddled with a name that sounds like a joke. Will Prity ever fit in?

Nadine Dreams of Home
BERNARD ASHLEY

Nadine finds Britain real scary. Not scary like soldiers, or burning buildings, or the sound of guns. But scary in other ways. If only her father were here with Nadine, her mother and her little brother. They have no idea if they will ever see Nadine's father again.

But then Nadine finds a special picture, and dreams a special dream ...

Mozart's Banana
GILLIAN CROSS

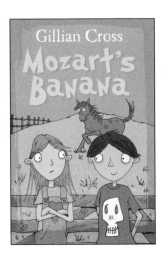

Mozart's Banana – a crazy name for a crazy horse. No one can tame Mozart's Banana. Even Sammy Foster failed, and he reckons he's the boss of the school. But then Alice Brett turns up. Alice is as cool as a choc-ice, and she isn't going to let anyone get the better of her, horse or boy ...

Gnomes, Gnomes, Gnomes
ANNE FINE

Sam's a bit obsessed. Any time he gets his hands on some clay, he makes gnomes. Dozens of them live out in the shed. But when Sam's mum needs that space, she says the gnomes will have to go. And so Sam plans a send-off for his little clay friends – a send-off that turns into a night the family will never forget!

More *4u2read* titles ...

How Brave Is That?
ANNE FINE

Tom's a brave lad. All he's ever wanted to do is work hard at school, pass his exams and join the army. He never gives up, even when terrible triplets turn his life upside down at home. But when disaster strikes on exam day, Tom has to come up with a plan. Fast. And it will be the bravest thing he has ever done!

The Haunting of Uncle Ron
ANNE FINE

Ian's not keen on Uncle Ron, the world's most boring visitor. Even the voices Uncle Ron hears from the 'Other Side' have nothing interesting to say. Ian can't stand it a moment longer. He must get rid of Uncle Ron. What he needs is a plan – and perhaps a helper ...

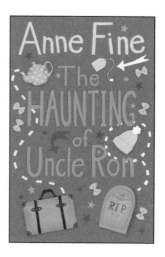

Mad Iris
JEREMY STRONG

Mad Iris doesn't like the ostrich farm. She likes Pudding Lane School much better! But the men from the ostrich farm are hot on her trail ...

Ross and Kate to the rescue!

Laugh your socks off with Jeremy Strong and the maddest ostrich on the planet!

Hostage
MALORIE BLACKMAN

"I'll make sure your dad never sees you again!"

Blindfolded. Alone. Angela has no idea where she is or what will happen next. The only thing she knows is she's been kidnapped. Is she brave enough to escape?

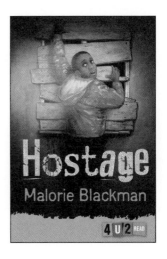

www.barringtonstoke.co.uk